This book is dedicated to YOU!

May you enjoy a lifetime of
dancing, music,
and letting your
imagination soar!

Cinderella

Princess Ballerinas

Created and Written by Megan Meyers
Edited and Illustrated by Joanna Jarc Robinson

Mia, Sofia, and Isabella paraded into dance class
with their pink outfits and big smiles.
"Hello, princess ballerinas!" said Miss Megan.
"I have a special adventure planned for today.
Has anyone ever heard of a princess named Cinderella?"

The ballerina's eyes lit up.
Of course they had heard of Cinderella!
Sometimes Miss Megan asked silly questions like that,
just to see if the girls were paying attention.

Miss Megan asked the girls to think about the story of
Cinderella. "Do you remember the handsome prince?"
The girls remembered.
"Well, we won't have a prince in our adventure."
Sofia joked, "Boys are stinky anyway." The girls giggled.

"Our story will be different." The girls were curious.
"Imagine and you will see," said Miss Megan.
"Be ready for few twists to the story you know.
Now close your eyes and repeat after me..."

If I close my eyes
and put my mind to it,
I can imagine!
There's nothing to it!

When they opened their eyes, they found themselves in a dark, dingy castle. There were cobwebs on the ceiling and dirt all over the floor. The room was filthy!

Miss Megan cupped her hand around her ear and imagined. "Do you hear those mean stepsisters?" she asked the girls. "Yes! They are saying, 'Cinderella, clean this house!" said Mia. "'Cinderella, bring me some tea,'" added Isabella. "Cinderella is so dirty, just look at her!' said Sofia.

"They were not very nice. Cinderella was kind to them anyway because she had a good heart," explained Miss Megan. "She cleaned the house without complaining. How did she clean?"

Sofia said, "She swept the floor!" The girls imagined and swept the floor with big graceful sweeps of their brooms. They swept left. Then they swept right. "That's called a balancé," explained Miss Megan.

Then Isabella said, "She washed the walls."
Mia added, "She brushed away the dust and
cobwebs, too." The princess ballerinas were
very graceful cleaners.

They balanced on one foot then the other as they moved around the room. "That's called passé," said Miss Megan.

Suddenly, Miss Megan listened again. "Now the stepsisters are talking about a dance. Hmmm..." The girls listened, too. "I want to go to the dance, but we are locked in this room," imagined Mia. "Who can help us?" wondered Sofia. "A fairy godmother!" shouted Isabella. And with that, Miss Megan pulled a magic wand from behind her back.

"I will be the fairy godmother. I will help you get to the dance. My wand is filled with magic sparkles. Spin in a circle and I will work my magic." The ballerinas spun around and around. Miss Megan sprinkled glittery sparkles on them and said, **"Spinnery sparkly, magical – woo**! Now, you are Miarella, Isabellarella, and Sofiarella." The girls thought those names sounded silly and cool at the same time.

"Now imagine a fancy gown.
Fix your hair just the way you like it.
You should look and feel your best. Be your best YOU,"
said Miss Megan.
"And don't forget those special slippers.
Point those toes - tendu."

The princess ballerinas were ready.
Everyone looked and felt great!

Then the princess ballerinas imagined a beautiful pink limo
and off they went to the dance!

They were so excited to arrive at the dance. The ballroom was beautiful! Miss Megan announced their names and each princess ballerina twirled across the dance floor.

The ballerinas noticed there were NO boys at the dance. They smiled. They didn't need boys to have fun.

Miss Megan taught
the princess ballerinas
a special dance
called a waltz.
It was fun
dancing
with friends!

They all danced their very best.
Nobody was the center of attention.
Each princess ballerina was amazing in her own way.

The ballerinas imagined the other girls
cheering for them. It was very encouraging.

Then Miss Megan invited all the girls to dance together. It was soooo much fun!

When the dance was over, there was no big wedding.
No end to the magic spell. No lost slipper.

Instead, the girls gathered in a circle on the floor.
Miss Megan said, "What did we learn about today?"
Mia said, "The waltz."
Next, Isabella said, "I learned that Cinderella was always
nice to everyone, even if they were mean to her. I don't
know how she did it. Maybe she practiced."
Sofia said, "I learned that it is good to look your best,
but it's more important to be nice
and have a good heart like Cinderella."
"Right! Be your best YOU," agreed Miss Megan.

Then Miss Megan gave them each as special heart bracelet,
and explained, "Remember, always keep a good heart.
Be your best you on the inside and out, just like Cinderella.

Now, "Spinnery sparkly, magical – woo! Goodbye!"
Miss Megan waved goodbye with her magic wand.
And with that, three smiling, sparkly, princess ballerinas
danced out the door.

Be your best YOU - inside and out!
To make the special heart bracelet:
1. Cut along the dotted lines.
2. Wrap around your wrist.
3. Tape the ends together.

Make a bracelet for a friend, too!

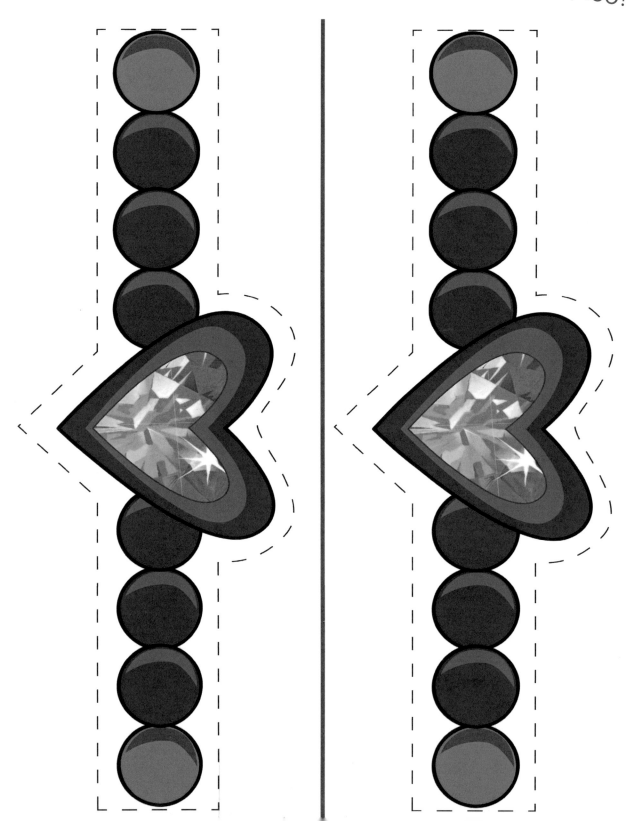

About Princess Ballerinas

History:
The Princess Ballerinas dance program is a <u>REAL</u> dance program created <u>JUST</u> for little ballerinas like Sofia, Mia, and Isabella, and your child, too!

Our passion is to inspire joy in children by providing a truly magical experience using the power of story, imagination, music, and dance.

To find a Princess Ballerina class near you, please visit
http://www.princessballerinas.com

41198871R20018